This Little Story
belongs to

_____

Published by Ladybird Books Ltd
80 Strand London WC2R 0RL
A Penguin Company

11 13 15 17 19 20 18 16 14 12

Illustrations © David Pace MCMXCVIII
© LADYBIRD BOOKS LTD MCMXCVIII

Printed in Italy

Clever Little Fairy

by Nicola Baxter
illustrated by David Pace

"I'm watching you, Bella Mirella," said the little fairy's mother, "and I can *see* that you're not practising. *Good girl, Tina Marina! Lovely dindins!*"

Bella Mirella made a face. "She's not even looking at me," she thought.

"I *am* looking at you and *don't* make that face," said her mother.

It was one of the big problems with having a mother who was a fairy – you couldn't be sure when she was using her magic.

And it was magic that was the problem now.

"You will be starting fairy school next week and you can't even do a simple doubling spell," said Bella Mirella's mother. "Now, try this apple."

Bella Mirella shut her eyes. She concentrated really hard. She *tried* to think of two shiny apples but it was hard when she felt so cross. Screwing up her face, she said the magic words:

"*Doubling spell,*
Work out well!"

PING!

"*Not* a great success," said her mother, looking at the two oranges.

"Let's go out into the garden now. But no playing for you, Bella Mirella. More practice!"

In the garden, there was no escape for Bella Mirella.

"Perhaps you are better at simple changing spells," said her mother. "Change this watering can into… er… a bucket. Concentrate!"

Bella Mirella looked hard at the watering can. She *tried* to imagine it losing its spout and handle. But just as she got ready to do the magic, Tina Marina started to yell. This time Bella Mirella shut her eyes *and* her ears, and said,
  "*Changing spell,*
  Work out well!"

PING!

"Bella Mirella, what are you *doing*?" her mother cried. "Poor little babykins!"

The little fairy *had* turned the watering can, but not into a bucket. Instead, she had turned it upside down!

"Oooh, did the nasty water fall on diddums' little head?" Bella Mirella's mother frowned at her oldest little fairy.

"You know, Bella Mirella, there are three kinds of spell that you must be able to do before you go to fairy school: doubling spells, changing spells and moving spells," she said.

"It seems that you can do them all – but not at the right time! Now just keep an eye on Tina Marina for me for two minutes while I get her a dry fairy suit. And practise!"

Bella Mirella sighed. She tried so hard with her spells but they just did not work out well. She looked at her sister. Some not-very-nice thoughts came into her head.

It's all your fault, little froggy face.

And the next second, without shutting her eyes, or saying the magic rhyme, or *anything*…

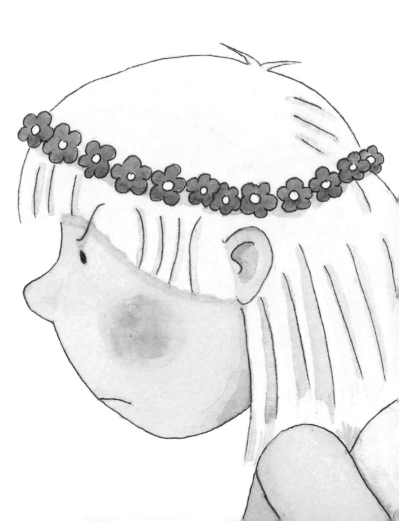

PING!

Tina Marina was a frog!

Bella Mirella was so shocked that she had to sit down. What had she done? And how?

"Oh no, this will mean double trouble," thought Bella Mirella.

And just as the words slipped through her mind…

PING!

There were *two* frogs!

Bella Mirella looked in horror at her *two* little green sisters. And just then she heard her mother coming back. She must hide the frogs while she thought of a plan! And as soon as she saw Tina Marina's pram...

PING!

The two frogs were safely
hidden away.

"Where's Tina Marina?" asked her
mother, looking around.

Bella Mirella was about to panic
when she suddenly realised how
easy it had all been. There was no
need to try really hard, or shut her
eyes, or say magic words. She just
had to be herself and think like
a fairy.

So with a secret smile, Bella Mirella
looked at the sky and…

PING!

Bella Mirella did a changing spell and a moving spell and an advanced reverse doubling spell all at once!

"Well, Bella Mirella," her mother smiled, "you are a *very* clever little fairy. I *knew* you could do it. You'll be able to teach Tina Marina soon."

But Bella Mirella thought to herself that she would wait until she was *quite* sure that Tina Marina had forgotten the day her toes were wiggly and green...